HENRY VAN DYKE CHRISTMAS CLASSICS COLLECTION

The Story of the Other Wise Man, The First Christmas Tree, & The Spirit of Christmas

HENRY VAN DYKE

CONTENTS

THE STORY OF THE OTHER WISE MAN

Who seeks for heaven alone to save his soul,
  May keep the path, but will not reach the goal;
  While he who walks in love may wander far,
  Yet God will bring him where the blessed are.

THE STORY OF THE OTHER
WISE MAN

You know the story of the Three Wise Men of the East, and how they travelled from far away to offer their gifts at the manger-cradle in Bethlehem. But have you ever heard the story of the Other Wise Man, who also saw the star in its rising, and set out to follow it, yet did not arrive with his brethren in the presence of the young child Jesus? Of the great desire of this fourth pilgrim, and how it was denied, yet accomplished in the denial; of his many wanderings and the probations of his soul; of the long way of his seeking, and the strange way of his finding, the One whom he sought—I would tell the tale as I have heard fragments of it in the Hall of Dreams, in the palace of the Heart of Man.

THE SIGN IN THE SKY

In the days when Augustus Caesar was master of many kings and Herod reigned in Jerusalem, there lived in the city of Ecbatana, among the mountains of Persia, a certain man named Artaban, the Median. His house stood close to the outermost of the seven walls which encircled the royal treasury. From his roof he could look over the rising battlements of black and white and crimson and blue and red and silver and gold, to the hill where the summer palace of the Parthian emperors glittered like a jewel in a sevenfold crown.

Around the dwelling of Artaban spread a fair garden, a tangle of flowers and fruit-trees, watered by a score of streams descending from the slopes of Mount Orontes, and made musical by innumerable birds. But all colour was lost in the soft and odorous darkness of the late September night, and all sounds were hushed in the deep charm of its silence, save the plashing of the water, like a voice half sobbing and half laughing under the shadows. High above the trees a dim glow of light shone through the curtained arches of the upper chamber, where the master of the house was holding council with his friends.

He stood by the doorway to greet his guests—a tall, dark man of about forty years, with brilliant eyes set near together under his broad brow, and firm lines graven around his fine, thin lips; the brow of a dreamer and the mouth of a soldier, a man of sensitive feeling but inflexible will—one of those who, in whatever age they may live, are born for inward conflict and a life of quest.

His robe was of pure white wool, thrown over a tunic of silk; and a white, pointed cap, with long lapels at the sides, rested on his flowing black hair. It was the dress of the ancient priesthood of the Magi, called the fire-worshippers.

"Welcome!" he said, in his low, pleasant voice, as one after another entered the room—"welcome, Abdus; peace be with you, Rhodaspes and Tigranes, and with you my father, Abgarus. You are all welcome, and this house grows bright with the joy of your presence."

There were nine of the men, differing widely in age, but alike in the richness of their dress of many-coloured silks, and in the massive golden collars around their necks, marking them as Parthian nobles, and in the winged circles of gold resting upon their breasts, the sign of the followers of Zoroaster.

They took their places around a small black altar at

the end of the room, where a tiny flame was burning.
Artaban, standing beside it, and waving a barsom of
thin tamarisk branches above the fire, fed it with dry
sticks of pine and fragrant oils. Then he began the
ancient chant of the Yasna, and the voices of his
companions joined in the beautiful hymn to Ahura-
Mazda:

We worship the Spirit Divine,
all wisdom and goodness possessing,
Surrounded by Holy Immortals,
the givers of bounty and blessing.
We joy in the works of His hands,
His truth and His power confessing.

We praise all the things that are pure,
for these are His only Creation;
The thoughts that are true, and the words
and deeds that have won approbation;
These are supported by Him,
and for these we make adoration.

Hear us, O Mazda! Thou livest
in truth and in heavenly gladness;
Cleanse us from falsehood, and keep us
from evil and bondage to badness;
Pour out the light and the joy of Thy life
on our darkness and sadness.

Shine on our gardens and fields,

Shine on our working and weaving;
Shine on the whole race of man,
Believing and unbelieving;
Shine on us now through the night,
Shine on us now in Thy might,
The flame of our holy love
and the song of our worship receiving.

The fire rose with the chant, throbbing as if it were made of musical flame, until it cast a bright illumination through the whole apartment, revealing its simplicity and splendour.

The floor was laid with tiles of dark blue veined with white; pilasters of twisted silver stood out against the blue walls; the clearstory of round-arched windows above them was hung with azure silk; the vaulted ceiling was a pavement of sapphires, like the body of heaven in its clearness, sown with silver stars. From the four corners of the roof hung four golden magic-wheels, called the tongues of the gods. At the eastern end, behind the altar, there were two dark-red pillars of porphyry; above them a lintel of the same stone, on which was carved the figure of a winged archer, with his arrow set to the string and his bow drawn.

The doorway between the pillars, which opened upon the terrace of the roof, was covered with a heavy curtain of the colour of a ripe pomegranate, embroidered with innumerable golden rays shooting upward from the floor. In effect the room was like a quiet, starry night, all azure and silver, flushed in the East with rosy promise of the dawn. It was, as the house of a man should be, an expression of the character and spirit of the master.

He turned to his friends when the song was ended, and invited them to be seated on the divan at the western end of the room.

"You have come to-night," said he, looking around the circle, "at my call, as the faithful scholars of Zoroaster, to renew your worship and rekindle your faith in the God of Purity, even as this fire has been rekindled on the altar. We worship not the fire, but Him of whom it is the chosen symbol, because it is the purest of all created things. It speaks to us of one who is Light and Truth. Is it not so, my father?"

"It is well said, my son," answered the venerable Abgarus. "The enlightened are never idolaters. They lift the veil of the form and go in to the shrine of the reality, and new light and truth are coming to them continually through the old symbols." "Hear me, then, my father and my friends," said Artaban, very quietly, "while I tell you of the new light and truth that have come to me through the most ancient of all signs. We have searched the secrets of nature together, and studied the healing virtues of water and fire and the plants. We have read also the books of prophecy in which the future is dimly foretold in words that are hard to understand. But the highest of all learning is the knowledge of the stars. To trace their courses is to untangle the threads of the mystery of life from the beginning to the end. If we could follow them perfectly, nothing would be hidden from us. But is not our knowledge of them still incomplete? Are there not many stars still beyond our horizon—lights that are known only to the dwellers in the far south-land, among the spice-trees of Punt and the gold mines of Ophir?"

There was a murmur of assent among the listeners.

"The stars," said Tigranes, "are the thoughts of the Eternal. They are numberless. But the thoughts of man can be counted, like the years of his life. The wisdom of the Magi is the greatest of all wisdoms on earth, because it knows its own ignorance. And that is the secret of power. We keep men always looking and waiting for a new sunrise. But we ourselves know that the darkness is equal to the light, and that the conflict between them will never be ended."

"That does not satisfy me," answered Artaban, "for, if the waiting must be endless, if there could be no fulfilment of it, then it would not be wisdom to look and wait. We should become like those new teachers of the Greeks, who say that there is no truth, and that the only wise men are those who spend their lives in discovering and exposing the lies that have been believed in the world. But the new sunrise will certainly dawn in the appointed time. Do not our own books tell us that this will come to pass, and that men will see the brightness of a great light?"

"That is true," said the voice of Abgarus; "every faithful disciple of Zoroaster knows the prophecy of the Avesta and carries the word in his heart. 'In that day Sosiosh the Victorious shall arise out of the number of the prophets in the east country. Around him shall shine a mighty brightness, and he shall make life everlasting, incorruptible, and immortal, and the dead shall rise again.'"

"This is a dark saying," said Tigranes, "and it may be that we shall never understand it. It is better to consider the things that are near at hand, and to increase the influence of the Magi in their own country, rather than to look for one who may be a stranger, and to whom we must resign our power."

The others seemed to approve these words. There was a silent feeling of agreement manifest among them; their looks responded with that indefinable expression which always follows when a speaker has uttered the thought that has been slumbering in the hearts of his listeners. But Artaban turned to Abgarus with a glow on his face, and said:

"My father, I have kept this prophecy in the secret place of my soul. Religion without a great hope would be like an altar without a living fire. And now the flame has burned more brightly, and by the light of it I have read other words which also have come from the fountain of Truth, and speak yet more clearly of the rising of the Victorious One in his brightness."

He drew from the breast of his tunic two small rolls of fine linen, with writing upon them, and unfolded them carefully upon his knee.

"In the years that are lost in the past, long before our fathers came into the land of Babylon, there were wise men in Chaldea, from whom the first of the Magi learned the secret of the heavens. And of these Balaam the son of Beor was one of the mightiest. Hear the words of his prophecy: 'There shall come a star out of Jacob, and a sceptre shall arise out of Israel.'"

The lips of Tigranes drew downward with contempt, as he said:

"Judah was a captive by the waters of Babylon, and the sons of Jacob were in bondage to our kings. The tribes of Israel are scattered through the mountains like lost sheep, and from the remnant that dwells in Judea under the yoke of Rome neither star nor sceptre shall arise."

"And yet," answered Artaban, "it was the Hebrew Daniel, the mighty searcher of dreams, the counsellor of kings, the wise Belteshazzar, who was most honored and beloved of our great King Cyrus. A prophet of sure things and a reader of the thoughts of God, Daniel proved himself to our people. And these are the words that he wrote." (Artaban read from the second roll:) "'Know, therefore, and understand that from the going forth of the commandment to restore Jerusalem, unto the Anointed One, the Prince, the time shall be seven and threescore and two weeks.'"

"But, my son," said Abgarus, doubtfully, "these are mystical numbers. Who can interpret them, or who can find the key that shall unlock their meaning?"

Artaban answered: "It has been shown to me and to my three companions among the Magi—Caspar, Melchior, and Balthazar. We have searched the ancient tablets of Chaldea and computed the time. It falls in this year. We have studied the sky, and in the spring of the year we saw two of the greatest stars draw near together in the sign of the Fish, which is the house of the Hebrews. We also saw a new star there, which shone for one night and then vanished. Now again the two great planets are meeting. This night is their conjunction. My three brothers are watching at the ancient temple of the Seven Spheres, at Borsippa, in Babylonia, and I am watching here. If the star shines again, they will wait ten days for me at the temple, and then we will set out together for Jerusalem, to see and worship the promised one who shall be born King of Israel. I believe the sign will come. I have made ready for the journey. I have sold my house and my possessions, and bought these three jewels—a sapphire, a ruby, and a pearl—to carry them as tribute to the King. And I ask you to go with me on the pilgrimage, that we may have joy together in finding the Prince who is worthy to be served."

While he was speaking he thrust his hand into the inmost fold of his girdle and drew out three great gems —one blue as a fragment of the night sky, one redder than a ray of sunrise, and one as pure as the peak of a snow mountain at twilight—and laid them on the outspread linen scrolls before him.

But his friends looked on with strange and alien eyes. A veil of doubt and mistrust came over their faces, like a fog creeping up from the marshes to hide the hills. They glanced at each other with looks of wonder and pity, as those who have listened to incredible sayings, the story of a wild vision, or the proposal of an impossible enterprise.

At last Tigranes said: "Artaban, this is a vain dream. It comes from too much looking upon the stars and the cherishing of lofty thoughts. It would be wiser to spend the time in gathering money for the new fire-temple at Chala. No king will ever rise from the broken race of Israel, and no end will ever come to the eternal strife of light and darkness. He who looks for it is a chaser of shadows. Farewell."

And another said: "Artaban, I have no knowledge of these things, and my office as guardian of the royal treasure binds me here. The quest is not for me. But if thou must follow it, fare thee well."

And another said: "In my house there sleeps a new bride, and I cannot leave her nor take her with me on this strange journey. This quest is not for me. But may thy steps be prospered wherever thou goest. So, farewell."

And another said: "I am ill and unfit for hardship, but there is a man among my servants whom I will send with thee when thou goest, to bring me word how thou farest."

But Abgarus, the oldest and the one who loved Artaban the best, lingered after the others had gone, and said, gravely: "My son, it may be that the light of truth is in this sign that has appeared in the skies, and then it will surely lead to the Prince and the mighty brightness. Or it may be that it is only a shadow of the light, as Tigranes has said, and then he who follows it will have only a long pilgrimage and an empty search. But it is better to follow even the shadow of the best than to remain content with the worst. And those who would see wonderful things must often be ready to travel alone. I am too old for this journey, but my heart shall be a companion of the pilgrimage day and night, and I shall know the end of thy quest. Go in peace."

So one by one they went out of the azure chamber with its silver stars, and Artaban was left in solitude.

He gathered up the jewels and replaced them in his girdle. For a long time he stood and watched the flame that flickered and sank upon the altar. Then he crossed the hall, lifted the heavy curtain, and passed out between the dull red pillars of porphyry to the terrace on the roof.

The shiver that thrills through the earth ere she rouses from her night sleep had already begun, and the cool wind that heralds the daybreak was drawing downward from the lofty snow-traced ravines of Mount Orontes. Birds, half awakened, crept and chirped among the rustling leaves, and the smell of ripened grapes came in brief wafts from the arbours.

Far over the eastern plain a white mist stretched like a lake. But where the distant peak of Zagros serrated the western horizon the sky was clear. Jupiter and Saturn rolled together like drops of lambent flame about to blend in one.

As Artaban watched them, behold, an azure spark was born out of the darkness beneath, rounding itself with purple splendours to a crimson sphere, and spiring upward through rays of saffron and orange into a point of white radiance. Tiny and infinitely remote, yet perfect in every part, it pulsated in the enormous vault as if the three jewels in the Magian's breast had mingled and been transformed into a living heart of light. He bowed his head. He covered his brow with his hands.

"It is the sign," he said. "The King is coming, and I will go to meet him."

BY THE WATERS OF BABYLON

All night long Vasda, the swiftest of Artaban's horses, had been waiting, saddled and bridled, in her stall, pawing the ground impatiently, and shaking her bit as if she shared the eagerness of her master's purpose, though she knew not its meaning.

Before the birds had fully roused to their strong, high, joyful chant of morning song, before the white mist had begun to lift lazily from the plain, the other wise man was in the saddle, riding swiftly along the high-road, which skirted the base of Mount Orontes, westward.

How close, how intimate is the comradeship between a man and his favourite horse on a long journey. It is a silent, comprehensive friendship, an intercourse beyond the need of words. They drink at the same way-side springs, and sleep under the same guardian stars. They are conscious together of the subduing spell of nightfall and the quickening joy of daybreak. The master shares his evening meal with his hungry companion, and feels the soft, moist lips caressing the palm of his hand as they close over the morsel of bread. In the gray dawn he is roused from his bivouac by the gentle stir of a warm, sweet breath over his sleeping face, and looks up into the eyes of his faithful fellow-traveller, ready and waiting for the toil of the day. Surely, unless he is a pagan and an unbeliever, by whatever name he calls upon his God, he will thank Him for this voiceless sympathy, this dumb affection, and his morning prayer will embrace a double blessing —God bless us both, and keep our feet from falling and our souls from death!

And then, through the keen morning air, the swift hoofs beat their spirited music along the road, keeping time to the pulsing of two hearts that are moved with the same eager desire—to conquer space, to devour the distance, to attain the goal of the journey.

Artaban must indeed ride wisely and well if he would keep the appointed hour with the other Magi; for the route was a hundred and fifty parasangs, and fifteen was the utmost that he could travel in a day. But he knew Vasda's strength, and pushed forward without anxiety, making the fixed distance every day, though he must travel late into the night, and in the morning long before sunrise.

He passed along the brown slopes of Mt. Orontes, furrowed by the rocky courses of a hundred torrents.

He crossed the level plains of the Nisaeans, where the famous herds of horses, feeding in the wide pastures, tossed their heads at Vasda's approach, and galloped away with a thunder of many hoofs, and flocks of wild birds rose suddenly from the swampy meadows, wheeling in great circles with a shining flutter of innumerable wings and shrill cries of surprise.

He traversed the fertile fields of Concabar, where the dust from the threshing-floors filled the air with a golden mist, half hiding the huge temple of Astarte with its four hundred pillars.

At Baghistan, among the rich gardens watered by fountains from the rock, he looked up at the mountain thrusting its immense rugged brow out over the road, and saw the figure of King Darius trampling upon his fallen foes, and the proud list of his wars and conquests graven high upon the face of the eternal cliff.

Over many a cold and desolate pass, crawling painfully across the wind-swept shoulders of the hills; down many a black mountain-gorge, where the river roared and raced before him like a savage guide; across many a smiling vale, with terraces of yellow limestone full of vines and fruit-trees; through the oak-groves of Carine and the dark Gates of Zagros, walled in by precipices; into the ancient city of Chala, where the people of Samaria had been kept in captivity long ago; and out again by the mighty portal, riven through the encircling hills, where he saw the image of the High Priest of the Magi sculptured on the wall of rock, with hand uplifted as if to bless the centuries of pilgrims; past the entrance of the narrow defile, filled from end to end with orchards of peaches and figs, through which the river Gyndes foamed down to meet him; over the broad rice-fields, where the autumnal vapours spread their deathly mists; following along the course of the river, under tremulous shadows of poplar and tamarind, among the lower hills; and out upon the flat plain, where the road ran straight as an arrow through the stubble-fields and parched meadows; past the city of Ctesiphon, where the Parthian emperors reigned, and the vast metropolis of Seleucia which Alexander built; across the swirling floods of Tigris and the many channels of Euphrates, flowing yellow through the corn-lands—Artaban pressed onward until he arrived, at nightfall of the tenth day, beneath the shattered walls of populous Babylon.

Vasda was almost spent, and he would gladly have turned into the city to find rest and refreshment for himself and for her. But he knew that it was three hours' journey yet to the Temple of the Seven Spheres, and he must reach the place by midnight if he would find his comrades waiting. So he did not halt, but rode steadily across the stubble-fields.

A grove of date-palms made an island of gloom in the pale yellow sea. As she passed into the shadow Vasda slackened her pace, and began to pick her way more carefully.

Near the farther end of the darkness an access of caution seemed to fall upon her. She scented some danger or difficulty; it was not in her heart to fly from it —only to be prepared for it, and to meet it wisely, as a good horse should do. The grove was close and silent as the tomb; not a leaf rustled, not a bird sang.

She felt her steps before her delicately, carrying her head low, and sighing now and then with apprehension. At last she gave a quick breath of anxiety and dismay, and stood stock-still, quivering in every muscle, before a dark object in the shadow of the last palm-tree.

Artaban dismounted. The dim starlight revealed the form of a man lying across the road. His humble dress and the outline of his haggard face showed that he was probably one of the poor Hebrew exiles who still dwelt in great numbers in the vicinity. His pallid skin, dry and yellow as parchment, bore the mark of the deadly fever which ravaged the marsh-lands in autumn. The chill of death was in his lean hand, and, as Artaban released it, the arm fell back inertly upon the motionless breast.

He turned away with a thought of pity, consigning the body to that strange burial which the Magians deem most fitting—the funeral of the desert, from which the kites and vultures rise on dark wings, and the beasts of prey slink furtively away, leaving only a heap of white bones in the sand.

But, as he turned, a long, faint, ghostly sigh came from the man's lips. The brown, bony fingers closed convulsively on the hem of the Magian's robe and held him fast.

Artaban's heart leaped to his throat, not with fear, but with a dumb resentment at the importunity of this blind delay. How could he stay here in the darkness to minister to a dying stranger? What claim had this unknown fragment of human life upon his compassion or his service? If he lingered but for an hour he could hardly reach Borsippa at the appointed time. His companions would think he had given up the journey. They would go without him. He would lose his quest.

But if he went on now, the man would surely die. If he stayed, life might be restored. His spirit throbbed and fluttered with the urgency of the crisis. Should he risk the great reward of his divine faith for the sake of a single deed of human love? Should he turn aside, if only for a moment, from the following of the star, to give a cup of cold water to a poor, perishing Hebrew?

"God of truth and purity," he prayed, "direct me in the holy path, the way of wisdom which Thou only knowest."

Then he turned back to the sick man. Loosening the grasp of his hand, he carried him to a little mound at the foot of the palm-tree. He unbound the thick folds of the turban and opened the garment above the sunken breast. He brought water from one of the small canals near by, and moistened the sufferer's brow and mouth. He mingled a draught of one of those simple but potent remedies which he carried always in his girdle—for the Magians were physicians as well as astrologers—and poured it slowly between the colourless lips. Hour after hour he labored as only a skilful healer of disease can do; and, at last, the man's strength returned; he sat up and looked about him.

"Who art thou?" he said, in the rude dialect of the

country, "and why hast thou sought me here to bring back my life?"

"I am Artaban the Magian, of the city of Ecbatana, and I am going to Jerusalem in search of one who is to be born King of the Jews, a great Prince and Deliverer for all men. I dare not delay any longer upon my journey, for the caravan that has waited for me may depart without me. But see, here is all that I have left of bread and wine, and here is a potion of healing herbs. When thy strength is restored thou can'st find the dwellings of the Hebrews among the houses of Babylon."

The Jew raised his trembling hands solemnly to heaven.

"Now may the God of Abraham and Isaac and Jacob bless and prosper the journey of the merciful, and bring him in peace to his desired haven. But stay; I have nothing to give thee in return—only this: that I can tell thee where the Messiah must be sought. For our prophets have said that he should be born not in Jerusalem, but in Bethlehem of Judah. May the Lord bring thee in safety to that place, because thou hast had pity upon the sick."

It was already long past midnight. Artaban rode in haste, and Vasda, restored by the brief rest, ran eagerly through the silent plain and swam the channels of the river. She put forth the remnant of her strength, and fled over the ground like a gazelle.

But the first beam of the sun sent her shadow before her as she entered upon the final stadium of the journey, and the eyes of Artaban anxiously scanning the great mound of Nimrod and the Temple of the Seven Spheres, could discern no trace of his friends.

The many-coloured terraces of black and orange and red and yellow and green and blue and white, shattered by the convulsions of nature, and crumbling under the repeated blows of human violence, still glittered like a ruined rainbow in the morning light.

Artaban rode swiftly around the hill. He dismounted and climbed to the highest terrace, looking out towards the west.

The huge desolation of the marshes stretched away to the horizon and the border of the desert. Bitterns stood by the stagnant pools and jackals skulked through the low bushes; but there was no sign of the caravan of the wise men, far or near.

At the edge of the terrace he saw a little cairn of broken bricks, and under them a piece of parchment. He caught it up and read: "We have waited past the midnight, and can delay no longer. We go to find the King. Follow us across the desert." Artaban sat down upon the ground and covered his head in despair.

"How can I cross the desert," said he, "with no food and with a spent horse? I must return to Babylon, sell my sapphire, and buy a train of camels, and provision for the journey. I may never overtake my friends. Only God the merciful knows whether I shall not lose the sight of the King because I tarried to show mercy."

FOR THE SAKE OF A LITTLE
CHILD

There was a silence in the Hall of Dreams, where I was listening to the story of the other wise man. And through this silence I saw, but very dimly, his figure passing over the dreary undulations of the desert, high upon the back of his camel, rocking steadily onward like a ship over the waves.

The land of death spread its cruel net around him. The stony wastes bore no fruit but briers and thorns. The dark ledges of rock thrust themselves above the surface here and there, like the bones of perished monsters. Arid and inhospitable mountain ranges rose before him, furrowed with dry channels of ancient torrents, white and ghastly as scars on the face of nature. Shifting hills of treacherous sand were heaped like tombs along the horizon. By day, the fierce heat pressed its intolerable burden on the quivering air; and no living creature moved, on the dumb, swooning earth, but tiny jerboas scuttling through the parched bushes, or lizards vanishing in the clefts of the rock. By night the jackals prowled and barked in the distance, and the lion made the black ravines echo with his hollow roaring, while a bitter, blighting chill followed the fever of the day. Through heat and cold, the Magian moved steadily onward.

Then I saw the gardens and orchards of Damascus, watered by the streams of Abana and Pharpar, with their sloping swards inlaid with bloom, and their thickets of myrrh and roses. I saw also the long, snowy ridge of Hermon, and the dark groves of cedars, and the valley of the Jordan, and the blue waters of the Lake of Galilee, and the fertile plain of Esdraelon, and the hills of Ephraim, and the highlands of Judah. Through all these I followed the figure of Artaban moving steadily onward, until he arrived at Bethlehem. And it was the third day after the three wise men had come to that place and had found Mary and Joseph, with the young child, Jesus, and had laid their gifts of gold and frankincense and myrrh at his feet.

Then the other wise man drew near, weary, but full of hope, bearing his ruby and his pearl to offer to the King. "For now at last," he said, "I shall surely find him, though it be alone, and later than my brethren. This is the place of which the Hebrew exile told me that the prophets had spoken, and here I shall behold the rising of the great light. But I must inquire about the visit of my brethren, and to what house the star directed them, and to whom they presented their tribute."

The streets of the village seemed to be deserted, and Artaban wondered whether the men had all gone up to the hill-pastures to bring down their sheep. From the open door of a low stone cottage he heard the sound of a woman's voice singing softly. He entered and found a young mother hushing her baby to rest. She told him of the strangers from the far East who had appeared in the village three days ago, and how they said that a star had guided them to the place where Joseph of Nazareth was lodging with his wife and her new-born child, and how they had paid reverence to the child and given him many rich gifts.

"But the travellers disappeared again," she continued, "as suddenly as they had come. We were afraid at the strangeness of their visit. We could not understand it. The man of Nazareth took the babe and his mother and fled away that same night secretly, and it was whispered that they were going far away to Egypt. Ever since, there has been a spell upon the village; something evil hangs over it. They say that the Roman soldiers are coming from Jerusalem to force a new tax from us, and the men have driven the flocks and herds far back among the hills, and hidden themselves to escape it."

Artaban listened to her gentle, timid speech, and the child in her arms looked up in his face and smiled, stretching out its rosy hands to grasp at the winged circle of gold on his breast. His heart warmed to the touch. It seemed like a greeting of love and trust to one who had journeyed long in loneliness and perplexity, fighting with his own doubts and fears, and following a light that was veiled in clouds.

"Might not this child have been the promised Prince?" he asked within himself, as he touched its soft cheek. "Kings have been born ere now in lowlier houses than this, and the favourite of the stars may rise even from a cottage. But it has not seemed good to the God of wisdom to reward my search so soon and so easily. The one whom I seek has gone before me; and now I must follow the King to Egypt."

The young mother laid the babe in its cradle, and rose to minister to the wants of the strange guest that fate had brought into her house. She set food before him, the plain fare of peasants, but willingly offered, and therefore full of refreshment for the soul as well as for the body. Artaban accepted it gratefully; and, as he ate, the child fell into a happy slumber, and murmured sweetly in its dreams, and a great peace filled the quiet room.

But suddenly there came the noise of a wild confusion and uproar in the streets of the village, a shrieking and wailing of women's voices, a clangor of brazen trumpets and a clashing of swords, and a desperate cry: "The soldiers! the soldiers of Herod! They are killing our children."

The young mother's face grew white with terror. She clasped her child to her bosom, and crouched motionless in the darkest corner of the room, covering him with the folds of her robe, lest he should wake and cry.

But Artaban went quickly and stood in the doorway of the house. His broad shoulders filled the portal from side to side, and the peak of his white cap all but touched the lintel.

The soldiers came hurrying down the street with bloody hands and dripping swords. At the sight of the stranger in his imposing dress they hesitated with surprise. The captain of the band approached the threshold to thrust him aside. But Artaban did not stir. His face was as calm as though he were watching the stars, and in his eyes there burned that steady radiance before which even the half-tamed hunting leopard shrinks, and the fierce bloodhound pauses in his leap. He held the soldier silently for an instant, and then said in a low voice:

"There is no one in this place but me, and I am waiting to give this jewel to the prudent captain who will leave me in peace."

He showed the ruby, glistening in the hollow of his hand like a great drop of blood.

The captain was amazed at the splendour of the gem. The pupils of his eyes expanded with desire, and the hard lines of greed wrinkled around his lips. He stretched out his hand and took the ruby.

"March on!" he cried to his men, "there is no child here. The house is still."

The clamour and the clang of arms passed down the street as the headlong fury of the chase sweeps by the secret covert where the trembling deer is hidden.

Artaban re-entered the cottage. He turned his face to the east and prayed:

"God of truth, forgive my sin! I have said the thing that is not, to save the life of a child. And two of my gifts are gone. I have spent for man that which was meant for God. Shall I ever be worthy to see the face of the King?"

But the voice of the woman, weeping for joy in the shadow behind him, said very gently:

"Because thou hast saved the life of my little one, may the Lord bless thee and keep thee; the Lord make His face to shine upon thee and be gracious unto thee; the Lord lift up His countenance upon thee and give thee peace."

IN THE HIDDEN WAY OF
SORROW

Then again there was a silence in the Hall of Dreams, deeper and more mysterious than the first interval, and I understood that the years of Artaban were flowing very swiftly under the stillness of that clinging fog, and I caught only a glimpse, here and there, of the river of his life shining through the shadows that concealed its course.

I saw him moving among the throngs of men in populous Egypt, seeking everywhere for traces of the household that had come down from Bethlehem, and finding them under the spreading sycamore-trees of Heliopolis, and beneath the walls of the Roman fortress of New Babylon beside the Nile—traces so faint and dim that they vanished before him continually, as footprints on the hard river-sand glisten for a moment with moisture and then disappear.

I saw him again at the foot of the pyramids, which lifted their sharp points into the intense saffron glow of the sunset sky, changeless monuments of the perishable glory and the imperishable hope of man. He looked up into the vast countenance of the crouching Sphinx and vainly tried to read the meaning of her calm eyes and smiling mouth. Was it, indeed, the mockery of all effort and all aspiration, as Tigranes had said—the cruel jest of a riddle that has no answer, a search that never can succeed? Or was there a touch of pity and encouragement in that inscrutable smile—a promise that even the defeated should attain a victory, and the disappointed should discover a prize, and the ignorant should be made wise, and the blind should see, and the wandering should come into the haven at last?

I saw him again in an obscure house of Alexandria, taking counsel with a Hebrew rabbi. The venerable man, bending over the rolls of parchment on which the prophecies of Israel were written, read aloud the pathetic words which foretold the sufferings of the promised Messiah—the despised and rejected of men, the man of sorrows and the acquaintance of grief.

"And remember, my son," said he, fixing his deep-set eyes upon the face of Artaban, "the King whom you are seeking is not to be found in a palace, nor among the rich and powerful. If the light of the world and the glory of Israel had been appointed to come with the greatness of earthly splendour, it must have appeared long ago. For no son of Abraham will ever again rival the power which Joseph had in the palaces of Egypt, or the magnificence of Solomon throned between the lions in Jerusalem. But the light for which the world is waiting is a new light, the glory that shall rise out of patient and triumphant suffering. And the kingdom which is to be established forever is a new kingdom, the royalty of perfect and unconquerable love. I do not know how this shall come to pass, nor how the turbulent kings and peoples of earth shall be brought to acknowledge the Messiah and pay homage to him. But this I know. Those who seek Him will do well to look among the poor and the lowly, the sorrowful and the oppressed."

So I saw the other wise man again and again, travelling from place to place, and searching among the people of the dispersion, with whom the little family from Bethlehem might, perhaps, have found a refuge. He passed through countries where famine lay heavy upon the land, and the poor were crying for bread. He made his dwelling in plague-stricken cities where the sick were languishing in the bitter companionship of helpless misery. He visited the oppressed and the afflicted in the gloom of subterranean prisons, and the crowded wretchedness of slave-markets, and the weary toil of galley-ships. In all this populous and intricate world of anguish, though he found none to worship, he found many to help. He fed the hungry, and clothed the naked, and healed the sick, and comforted the captive; and his years went by more swiftly than the weaver's shuttle that flashes back and forth through the loom while the web grows and the invisible pattern is completed.

It seemed almost as if he had forgotten his quest.

But once I saw him for a moment as he stood alone at sunrise, waiting at the gate of a Roman prison. He had taken from a secret resting-place in his bosom the pearl, the last of his jewels. As he looked at it, a mellower lustre, a soft and iridescent light, full of shifting gleams of azure and rose, trembled upon its surface. It seemed to have absorbed some reflection of the colours of the lost sapphire and ruby. So the profound, secret purpose of a noble life draws into itself the memories of past joy and past sorrow. All that has helped it, all that has hindered it, is transfused by a subtle magic into its very essence. It becomes more luminous and precious the longer it is carried close to the warmth of the beating heart. Then, at last, while I was thinking of this pearl, and of its meaning, I heard the end of the story of the other wise man.

A PEARL OF GREAT PRICE

Three-and-thirty years of the life of Artaban had passed away, and he was still a pilgrim and a seeker after light. His hair, once darker than the cliffs of Zagros, was now white as the wintry snow that covered them. His eyes, that once flashed like flames of fire, were dull as embers smouldering among the ashes.

Worn and weary and ready to die, but still looking for the King, he had come for the last time to Jerusalem. He had often visited the holy city before, and had searched through all its lanes and crowded hovels and black prisons without finding any trace of the family of Nazarenes who had fled from Bethlehem long ago. But now it seemed as if he must make one more effort, and something whispered in his heart that, at last, he might succeed. It was the season of the Passover. The city was thronged with strangers. The children of Israel, scattered in far lands all over the world, had returned to the Temple for the great feast, and there had been a confusion of tongues in the narrow streets for many days.

But on this day there was a singular agitation visible in the multitude. The sky was veiled with a portentous gloom, and currents of excitement seemed to flash through the crowd like the thrill which shakes the forest on the eve of a storm. A secret tide was sweeping them all one way. The clatter of sandals, and the soft, thick sound of thousands of bare feet shuffling over the stones, flowed unceasingly along the street that leads to the Damascus gate.

Artaban joined company with a group of people from his own country, Parthian Jews who had come up to keep the Passover, and inquired of them the cause of the tumult, and where they were going.

"We are going," they answered, "to the place called Golgotha, outside the city walls, where there is to be an execution. Have you not heard what has happened? Two famous robbers are to be crucified, and with them another, called Jesus of Nazareth, a man who has done many wonderful works among the people, so that they love him greatly. But the priests and elders have said that he must die, because he gave himself out to be the Son of God. And Pilate has sent him to the cross because he said that he was the 'King of the Jews.'"

How strangely these familiar words fell upon the tired heart of Artaban! They had led him for a lifetime over land and sea. And now they came to him darkly and mysteriously like a message of despair. The King had arisen, but he had been denied and cast out. He was about to perish. Perhaps he was already dying. Could it be the same who had been born in Bethlehem, thirty-three years ago, at whose birth the star had appeared in heaven, and of whose coming the prophets had spoken?

Artaban's heart beat unsteadily with that troubled, doubtful apprehension which is the excitement of old age. But he said within himself, "The ways of God are stranger than the thoughts of men, and it may be that I shall find the King, at last, in the hands of His enemies, and shall come in time to offer my pearl for His ransom before He dies."

So the old man followed the multitude with slow and painful steps towards the Damascus gate of the city. Just beyond the entrance of the guard-house a troop of Macedonian soldiers came down the street, dragging a young girl with torn dress and dishevelled hair. As the Magian paused to look at her with compassion, she broke suddenly from the hands of her tormentors, and threw herself at his feet, clasping him around the knees. She had seen his white cap and the winged circle on his breast.

"Have pity on me," she cried, "and save me, for the sake of the God of Purity! I also am a daughter of the true religion which is taught by the Magi. My father was a merchant of Parthia, but he is dead, and I am seized for his debts to be sold as a slave. Save me from worse than death!"

Artaban trembled.

It was the old conflict in his soul, which had come

to him in the palm-grove of Babylon and in the cottage at Bethlehem—the conflict between the expectation of faith and the impulse of love. Twice the gift which he had consecrated to the worship of religion had been drawn from his hand to the service of humanity. This was the third trial, the ultimate probation, the final and irrevocable choice.

Was it his great opportunity, or his last temptation? He could not tell. One thing only was clear in the darkness of his mind—it was inevitable. And does not the inevitable come from God?

One thing only was sure to his divided heart—to rescue this helpless girl would be a true deed of love. And is not love the light of the soul?

He took the pearl from his bosom. Never had it seemed so luminous, so radiant, so full of tender, living lustre. He laid it in the hand of the slave.

"This is thy ransom, daughter! It is the last of my treasures which I kept for the King."

While he spoke the darkness of the sky thickened, and shuddering tremors ran through the earth, heaving convulsively like the breast of one who struggles with mighty grief.

The walls of the houses rocked to and fro. Stones were loosened and crashed into the street. Dust clouds filled the air. The soldiers fled in terror, reeling like drunken men. But Artaban and the girl whom he had ransomed crouched helpless beneath the wall of the Praetorium.

What had he to fear? What had he to live for? He

had given away the last remnant of his tribute for the King. He had parted with the last hope of finding Him. The quest was over, and it had failed. But, even in that thought, accepted and embraced, there was peace. It was not resignation. It was not submission. It was something more profound and searching. He knew that all was well, because he had done the best that he could, from day to day. He had been true to the light that had been given to him. He had looked for more. And if he had not found it, if a failure was all that came out of his life, doubtless that was the best that was possible. He had not seen the revelation of "life everlasting, incorruptible and immortal." But he knew that even if he could live his earthly life over again, it could not be otherwise than it had been.

One more lingering pulsation of the earthquake quivered through the ground. A heavy tile, shaken from the roof, fell and struck the old man on the temple. He lay breathless and pale, with his gray head resting on the young girl's shoulder, and the blood trickling from the wound. As she bent over him, fearing that he was dead, there came a voice through the twilight, very small and still, like music sounding from a distance, in which the notes are clear but the words are lost. The girl turned to see if some one had spoken from the window above them, but she saw no one.

Then the old man's lips began to move, as if in answer, and she heard him say in the Parthian tongue:

"Not so, my Lord! For when saw I thee an hungered, and fed thee? Or thirsty, and gave thee drink? When saw I thee a stranger, and took thee in? Or naked, and clothed thee? When saw I thee sick or in prison, and came unto thee? Three-and-thirty years have I looked for thee; but I have never seen thy face, nor ministered to thee, my King."

He ceased, and the sweet voice came again. And again the maid heard it, very faintly and far away. But now it seemed as though she understood the words:

"Verily I say unto thee, inasmuch as thou hast done it unto one of the least of these my brethren, thou hast done it unto me."

A calm radiance of wonder and joy lighted the pale face of Artaban like the first ray of dawn on a snowy mountain-peak. One long, last breath of relief exhaled gently from his lips.

His journey was ended. His treasures were accepted. The other Wise Man had found the King.

THE FIRST CHRISTMAS
TREE

❧ I ❧
THE CALL OF THE WOODSMAN

The day before Christmas, in the year of our Lord 722.

Broad snow-meadows glistening white along the banks of the river Moselle; pallid hill-sides blooming with mystic roses where the glow of the setting sun still lingered upon them; an arch of clearest, faintest azure bending overhead; in the center of the aerial landscape of the massive walls of the cloister of Pfalzel, gray to the east, purple to the west; silence over all,—a gentle, eager, conscious stillness, diffused through the air like perfume, as if earth and sky were hushing themselves to hear the voice of the river faintly murmuring down the valley.

In the cloister, too, there was silence at the sunset hour. All day long there had been a strange and joyful stir among the nuns. A breeze of curiosity and excitement had swept along the corridors and through every quiet cell.

The elder sisters,—the provost, the deaconess, the

stewardess, the portress with her huge bunch of keys jingling at her girdle,—had been hurrying to and fro, busied with household cares. In the huge kitchen there was a bustle of hospitable preparation. The little bandy-legged dogs that kept the spits turning before the fires had been trotting steadily for many an hour, until their tongues hung out for want of breath. The big black pots swinging from the cranes had bubbled and gurgled and shaken and sent out puffs of appetizing steam.

St. Martha was in her element. It was a field-day for her virtues.

The younger sisters, the pupils of the convent, had forsaken their Latin books and their embroidery-frames, their manuscripts and their miniatures, and fluttered through the halls in little flocks like merry snow-birds, all in black and white, chattering and whispering together. This was no day for tedious task-work, no day for grammar or arithmetic, no day for picking out illuminated letters in red and gold on stiff parchment, or patiently chasing intricate patterns over thick cloth with the slow needle. It was a holiday. A famous visitor had come to the convent.

It was Winfried of England, whose name in the Roman tongue was Boniface, and whom men called the Apostle of Germany. A great preacher; a wonderful scholar; he had written a Latin grammar himself,—think of it,—and he could hardly sleep without a book under his pillow; but, more than all, a great and daring traveller, a venturesome pilgrim, a high-priest of romance.

He had left his home and his fair estate in Wessex; he would not stay in the rich monastery of Nutescelle, even though they had chosen him as the abbot; he had refused a bishopric at the court of King Karl. Nothing would content him but to go out into the wild woods and preach to the heathen.

Up and down through the forests of Hesse and Thuringia, and along the borders of Saxony, he had wandered for years, with a handful of companions, sleeping under the trees, crossing mountains and marshes, now here, now there, never satisfied with ease and comfort, always in love with hardship and danger.

What a man he was! Fair and slight, but straight as a spear and strong as an oaken staff. His face was still young; the smooth skin was bronzed by wing and sun. His gray eyes, clear and kind, flashed like fire when he spoke of his adventures, and of the evil deeds of the false priests with whom he had contended.

What tales he had told that day! Not of miracles wrought by sacred relics; nor of courts and councils and splendid cathedrals; though he knew much of these things, and had been at Rome and received the Pope's blessing. But to-day he had spoken of long journeyings by sea and land; of perils by fire and flood; of wolves and bears and fierce snowstorms and black nights in the lonely forest; of dark altars of heaven gods, and weird, bloody sacrifices, and narrow escapes from wandering savages.

The little novices had gathered around him, and their faces had grown pale and their eyes bright as they listened with parted lips, entranced in admiration, twining their arms about one another's shoulders and holding closely together, half in fear, half in delight. The older nuns had turned from their tasks and paused, in passing by, to hear the pilgrim's story. Too well they knew the truth of what he spoke. Many a one among them had seen the smoke rising from the ruins of her father's roof. Many a one had a brother far away in the wild country to whom her heart went out night and day, wondering if he were still among the living.

But now the excitements of that wonderful day were over; the hours of the evening meal had come; the inmates of the cloister were assembled in the refectory.

On the dais sat the stately Abbess Addula, daughter of King Dagobert, looking a princess indeed, in her violet tunic, with the hood and cuffs of her long white robe trimmed with fur, and a snowy veil resting like a crown on her snowy hair. At her right hand was the honoured guest, and at her left hand her grandson, the young Prince Gregor, a big, manly boy, just returned from school.

The long, shadowy hall, with its dark-brown raters and beams; the double rows of nuns, with their pure veils and fair faces; the ruddy flow of the slanting sunbeams striking upwards through the tops of the windows and painting a pink glow high up on the walls, —it was all as beautiful as a picture, and as silent. For this was the rule of the cloister, that at the table all should sit in stillness for a little while, and then one should read aloud, while the rest listened.

"It is the turn of my grandson to read to-day," said the abbess to Winfried; "we shall see how much he has learned in the school. Read, Gregor; the place in the book is marked."

The tall lad rose from his seat and turned the pages of the manuscript. It was a copy of Jerome's version of the Scriptures in Latin, and the marked place was in the letter of St. Paul to the Ephesians,—the passage where he describes the preparation of the Christian as the arming of a warrior for glorious battle. The young voice rang out clearly, rolling the sonorous words, without slip or stumbling, to the end of the chapter.

Winfried listened, smiling. "My son," said he, as the reader paused, "that was bravely read. Understandest thou what thou readest?"

"Surely, father," answered the boy; "it was taught me by the masters at Treves; and we have read this epistle clear through, from beginning to end, so that I almost know it by heart."

Then he began again to repeat the passage, turning away from the page as if to show his skill.

But Winfried stopped him with a friendly lifting of the hand.

"No so, my son; that was not my meaning. When we pray, we speak to God; when we read, it is God who speaks to us. I ask whether thou hast heard what He has said to thee, in thine own words, in the common speech. Come, give us again the message of the warrior and his armour and his battle, in the mother-tongue, so that all can understand it."

The boy hesitated, blushed, stammered; then he came around to Winfried's seat, bringing the book. "Take the book, my father," he cried, "and read it for me. I cannot see the meaning plain, though I love the sound of the words. Religion I know, and the doctrines of our faith, and the life of priests and nuns in the cloister, for which my grandmother designs me, though it likes me little. And fighting I know, and the life of warriors and heroes, for I have read of it in Virgil and the ancients, and heard a bit from the soldiers at Treves; and I would fain taste more of it, for it likes me much. But how the two lives fit together, or what need there is of armour for a clerk in holy orders, I can never see. Tell me the meaning, for if there is a man in all the world that knows it, I am sure it is none other than thou."

So Winfried took the book and closed it, clasping the boy's hand with his own.

"Let us first dismiss the others to their vespers," said he, "lest they should be weary."

A sign from the abbess; a chanted benediction; a murmuring of sweet voices and a soft rustling of many feet over the rushes on the floor; the gentle tide of noise flowed out through the doors and ebbed away down the corridors; the three at the head of the table were left alone in the darkening room.

Then Winfried began to translate the parable of the soldier into the realities of life.

At every turn he knew how to flash a new light into the picture out of his own experience. He spoke of the combat with self, and of the wrestling with dark spirits in solitude. He spoke of the demons that men had worshipped for centuries in the wilderness, and whose malice they invoked against the stranger who ventured into the gloomy forest. Gods, they called them, and told strange tales of their dwelling among the impenetrable branches of the oldest trees and in the caverns of the shaggy hills; of their riding on the wind-horses and hurling spears of lightning against their foes. Gods they were not, but foul spirits of the air, rulers of the darkness. Was there not glory and honour in fighting with them, in daring their anger under the shield of faith, in putting them to flight with the sword of truth? What better adventure could a brave man ask than to go forth against them, and wrestle with them, and conquer them?

"Look you, my friends," said Winfried, "how sweet and peaceful is this convent to-night, on the eve of the nativity of the Prince of Peace! It is a garden full of flowers in the heart of winter; a nest among the branches of a great tree shaken by the winds; a still haven on the edge of a tempestuous sea. And this is what religion means for those who are chosen and called to quietude and prayer and meditation.

"But out yonder in the wide forest, who knows what storms are raving to-night in the hearts of men, though all the woods are still? who knows what haunts of wrath and cruelty and fear are closed to-night against the advent of the Prince of Peace? And shall I tell you what religion means to those who are called and chosen to dare and to fight, and to conquer the world for Christ? It means to launch out into the deep. It means to go against the strongholds of the adversary. It means to struggle to win an entrance for their Master everywhere. What helmet is strong enough for this strife save the helmet of salvation? What breastplate can guard a man against these fiery darts but the breastplate of righteousness? What shoes can stand the wear of these journeys but the preparation of the gospel of peace?"

"Shoes?" he cried again, and laughed as if a sudden thought had struck him. He thrust out his foot, covered with a heavy cowhide boot, laced high about his leg with thongs of skin.

"See here,—how a fighting man of the cross is shod! I have seen the boots of the Bishop of Tours,— white kid, broidered with silk; a day in the bogs would tear them to shreds. I have seen the sandals that the monks use on the highroads,—yes, and worn them; ten pair of them have I worn out and thrown away in a single journey. Now I shoe my feet with the toughest hides, hard as iron; no rock can cut them, no branches can tear them. Yet more than one pair of these have I outworn, and many more shall I outwear ere my journeys are ended. And I think, if God is gracious to me, that I shall die wearing them. Better so than in a soft bed with silken coverings. The boots of a warrior, a hunter, a woodsman,—these are my preparation of the gospel of peace."

"Come, Gregor," he said, laying his brown hand on the youth's shoulder, "come, wear the forester's boots with me. This is the life to which we are called. Be strong in the Lord, a hunter of the demons, a subduer of the wilderness, a woodsman of the faith. Come!"

The boy's eyes sparkled. He turned to his grand-mother. She shook her head vigorously.

"Nay, father," she said, "draw not the lad away from my side with these wild words. I need him to help me with my labours, to cheer my old age."

"Do you need him more than the Master does?" asked Winfried; "and will you take the wood that is fit for a bow to make a distaff?"

"But I fear for the child. Thy life is too hard for him. He will perish with hunger in the woods."

"Once," said Winfried, smiling, "we were camped by the bank of the river Ohru. The table was spread for the morning meal, but my comrades cried that it was empty; the provisions were exhausted; we must go without breakfast, and perhaps starve before we could escape from the wilderness. While they complained, a fish-hawk flew up from the river with flapping wings, and let fall a great pike in the midst of the camp. There was food enough and to spare. Never have I seen the righteous forsaken, nor his seed begging bread."

"But the fierce pagans of the forest," cried the abbess,—"they may pierce the boy with their arrows, or dash out his brains with their axes. He is but a child, too young for the dangers of strife."

"A child in years," replied Winfried, "but a man in

spirit. And if the hero must fall early in the battle, he wears the brighter crown, not a leaf withered, not a flower fallen."

The aged princess trembled a little. She drew Gregor close to her side, and laid her hand gently on his brown hair.

"I am not sure that he wants to leave me yet. Besides, there is no horse in the stable to give him, now, and he cannot go as befits the grandson of a king."

Gregor looked straight into her eyes.

"Grandmother," said he, "dear grandmother, if thou wilt not give me a horse to ride with this man of God, I will go with him afoot."

II

THE TRAIL THROUGH THE FOREST

Two years had passed, to a day, almost to an hour, since that Christmas eve in the cloister of Pfalzel. A little company of pilgrims, less than a score a men, were creeping slowly northward through the wide forest that rolled over the hills of central Germany.

At the head of the band marched Winfried, clad in a tunic of fur, with his long black robe girt high about his waist, so that it might not hinder his stride. His hunter's boots were crusted with snow. Drops of ice sparkled like jewels along the thongs that bound his legs. There was no other ornament to his dress except the bishop's cross hanging on his breast, and the broad silver clasp that fastened his cloak about his neck. He carried a strong, tall staff in his hand, fashioned at the top into the form of a cross.

Close beside him, keeping step like a familiar comrade, was the young Prince Gregor. Long marches through the wilderness had stretched his limbs and broadened his back, and made a man of him in stature as well as in spirit. His jacket and cap were of wolfskin, and on his shoulder he carried an axe, with broad, shining blade. He was a mighty woodsman now, and could make a spray of chips fly around him as he hewed his way through the trunk of spruce-tree.

Behind these leaders followed a pair of teamsters, guiding a rude sledge, loaded with food and the equipage of the camp, and drawn by two big, shaggy horses, blowing thick clouds of steam from their frosty nostrils. Tiny icicles hung from the hairs on their lips. Their flanks were smoking. They sank above the fetlocks at every step in the soft snow.

Last of all came the rear guard, armed with bows and javelins. It was no child's play, in those days, to cross Europe afoot.

The weird woodland, sombre and illimitable, covered hill and vale, tableland and mountain-peak. There were wide moors where the wolves hunted in packs as if the devil drove them, and tangled thickets where the lynx and the boar made their lairs. Fierce bears lurked among the rocky passes, and had not yet learned to fear the face of man. The gloomy recesses of the forest gave shelter to inhabitants who were still more cruel and dangerous than beasts of prey,— outlaws and sturdy robbers and mad were-wolves and bands of wandering pillagers.

The pilgrim who would pass from the mouth of the Tiber to the mouth of the Rhine must travel with a little army of retainers, or else trust in God and keep his arrows loose in the quiver.

The travellers were surrounded by an ocean of trees, so vast, so full of endless billows, that it seemed to be pressing on every side to overwhelm them. Gnarled oaks, with branches twisted and knotted as if in rage, rose in groves like tidal waves. Smooth forests of beech-trees, round and gray, swept over the knolls and slopes of land in a mighty ground-swell. But most of all, the multitude of pines and firs, innumerable and monotonous, with straight, stark trunks, and branches woven together in an unbroken Hood of darkest green, crowded through the valleys and over the hills, rising on the highest ridges into ragged crests, like the foaming edge of breakers.

Through this sea of shadows ran a narrow stream of shining whiteness,—an ancient Roman road, covered with snow. It was as if some great ship had ploughed through the green ocean long ago, and left behind it a thick, smooth wake of foam. Along this open track the travellers held their way,—heavily, for the drifts were deep; warily, for the hard winter had driven many packs of wolves down from the moors.

The steps of the pilgrims were noiseless; but the sledges creaked over the dry snow, and the panting of the horses throbbed through the still, cold air. The pale-blue shadows on the western side of the road grew longer. The sun, declining through its shallow arch, dropped behind the tree-tops. Darkness followed swiftly, as if it had been a bird of prey waiting for this sign to swoop down upon the world.

"Father," said Gregor to the leader, "surely this day's march is done. It is time to rest, and eat, and sleep. If we press onward now, we cannot see our steps; and will not that be against the word of the psalmist David, who bids us not to put confidence in the legs of a man?"

Winfried laughed. "Nay, my son Gregor," said he, "thou hast tripped, even now, upon thy text. For David said only, 'I take no pleasure in the legs of a man.' And so say I, for I am not minded to spare thy legs or mine, until we come farther on our way, and do what must be done this night. Draw the belt tighter, my son, and hew me out this tree that is fallen across the road, for our campground is not here."

The youth obeyed; two of the foresters sprang to help him; and while the soft fir-wood yielded to the stroke of the axes, and the snow flew from the bending branches, Winfried turned and spoke to his followers in a cheerful voice, that refreshed them like wine.

"Courage, brothers, and forward yet a little! The moon will light us presently, and the path is plain. Well know I that the journey is weary; and my own heart wearies also for the home in England, where those I love are keeping feast this Christmas eve. But we have work to do before we feast to-night. For this is the Yuletide, and the heathen people of the forest have gathered at the thunder-oak of Geismar to worship their god, Thor. Strange things will be seen there, and deeds which make the soul black. But we are sent to lighten their darkness; and we will teach our kinsmen to keep a Christmas with us such as the woodland has never known. Forward, then, and let us stiffen up our feeble knees!"

A murmur of assent came from the men. Even the horses seemed to take fresh heart. They flattened their backs to draw the heavy loads, and blew the frost from their nostrils as they pushed ahead.

The night grew broader and less oppressive. A gate of brightness was opened secretly somewhere in the sky; higher and higher swelled the clear moon-flood, until it poured over the eastern wall of forest into the road. A drove of wolves howled faintly in the distance, but they were receding, and the sound soon died away. The stars sparkled merrily through the stringent air; the small, round moon shone like silver; little breaths of the dreaming wind wandered whispering across the pointed fir-tops, as the pilgrims toiled bravely onward, following their clue of light through a labyrinth of darkness.

After a while the road began to open out a little. There were spaces of meadow-land, fringed with alders, behind which a boisterous river ran, clashing through spears of ice.

Rude houses of hewn logs appeared in the openings, each one casting a patch of inky blackness upon the snow. Then the travellers passed a larger group of dwellings, all silent and unlighted; and beyond, they saw a great house, with many outbuildings and enclosed courtyards, from which the hounds bayed furiously, and a noise of stamping horses came from the stalls. But there was no other sound of life. The fields around lay bare to the moon. They saw no man, except that once, on a path that skirted the farther edge of a meadow, three dark figures passed by, running very swiftly.

Then the road plunged again into a dense thicket, traversed it, and climbing to the left, emerged suddenly upon a glade, round and level except at the northern side, where a swelling hillock was crowned with a huge oak-tree. It towered above the heath, a giant with contorted arms, beckoning to the host of lesser trees. "Here," cried Winfried, as his eyes flashed and his hand lifted his heavy staff, "here is the Thunder-oak; and here the cross of Christ shall break the hammer of the false god Thor."

III

THE SHADOW OF THE THUNDER-OAK

3

Withered leaves still clung to the branches of the oak: torn and faded banners of the departed summer. The bright crimson of autumn had long since disappeared, bleached away by the storms and the cold. But to-night these tattered remnants of glory were red again: ancient bloodstains against the dark-blue sky. For an immense fire had been kindled in front of the tree. Tongues of ruddy flame, fountains of ruby sparks, ascended through the spreading limbs and flung a fierce illumination upward and around. ward and around. The pale, pure moonlight that bathed the surrounding forests was quenched and eclipsed here. Not a beam of it sifted down-ward through the branches of the oak. It stood like a pillar of cloud between the still light of heaven and the crackling, flashing fire of earth.

But the fire itself was invisible to Winfried and his companions. A great throng of people were gathered around it in a half-circle, their backs to the open glade, their faces towards the oak. Seen against that glowing background, it was but the silhouette of a crowd, vague, black, formless, mysterious.

The travellers paused for a moment at the edge of the thicket, and took counsel together.

"It is the assembly of the tribe," said one of the foresters, "the great night of the council. I heard of it three days ago, as we passed through one of the villages. All who swear by the old gods have been summoned. They will sacrifice a steed to the god of war, and drink blood, and eat horse-flesh to make them strong. It will be at the peril of our lives if we approach them. At least we must hide the cross, if we would escape death."

"Hide me no cross," cried Winfried, lifting his staff, "for I have come to show it, and to make these blind folk see its power. There is more to be done here to-night than the slaying of a steed, and a greater evil to be stayed than the shameful eating of meat sacrificed to idols. I have seen it in a dream. Here the cross must stand and be our rede."

At his command the sledge was left in the border of the wood, with two of the men to guard it, and the rest of the company moved forward across the open ground. They approached unnoticed, for all the multitude were looking intently towards the fire at the foot of the oak.

Then Winfried's voice rang out, "Hail, ye sons of

the forest! A stranger claims the warmth of your fire in the winter night."

Swiftly, and as with a single motion, a thousand eyes were bent upon the speaker. The semicircle opened silently in the middle; Winfried entered with his followers; it closed again behind them.

Then, as they looked round the curving ranks, they saw that the hue of the assemblage was not black, but white,—dazzling, radiant, solemn. White, the robes of the women clustered together at the points of the wide crescent; white, the glittering byrnies of the warriors standing in close ranks; white, the fur mantles of the aged men who held the central place in the circle; white, with the shimmer of silver ornaments and the purity of lamb's-wool, the raiment of a little group of children who stood close by the fire; white, with awe and fear, the faces of all who looked at them; and over all the flickering, dancing radiance of the flames played and glimmered like a faint, vanishing tinge of blood on snow.

The only figure untouched by the glow was the old priest, Hunrad, with his long, spectral robe, flowing hair and beard, and dead-pale face, who stood with his back to the fire and advanced slowly to meet the strangers.

"Who are you? Whence come you, and what seek you here?" His voice was heavy and toneless as a muffled bell.

"You kinsman am I, of the German brotherhood," answered Winfried, "and from England, beyond the sea, have I come to bring you a greeting from that land, and a message from the All-Father, whose servant I am."

"Welcome, then," said Hunrad, "welcome, kinsman, and be silent; for what passes here is too high to wait, and must be done before the moon crosses the middle heaven, unless, indeed, thou hast some sign or token from the gods. Canst thou work miracles?"

The question came sharply, as if a sudden gleam of hope had flashed through the tangle of the old priest's mind. But Winfried's voice sank lower and a cloud of disappointment passed over his face as he replied: "Nay, miracles have I never wrought, though I have heard of many; but the All-Father has given no power to my hands save such as belongs to common man."

"Stand still, then, thou common man," said Hunrad, scornfully, "and behold what the gods have called us hither to do. This night is the death-night of the sun-god, Baldur the Beautiful, beloved of gods and men. This night is the hour of darkness and the power of winter, of sacrifice and mighty fear. This night the great Thor, the god of thunder and war, to whom this oak is sacred, is grieved for the death of Baldur, and angry with this people because they have forsaken his worship. Long is it since an offering has been laid upon his altar, long since the roots of his holy tree have been fed with blood. Therefore its leaves have withered before the time, and its boughs are heavy with death. Therefore the Slavs and the Wends have beaten us in battle. Therefore the harvests have failed, and the wolfhordes have ravaged the folds, and the strength has departed from the bow, and the wood of the spear has broken, and the wild boar has slain the huntsman. Therefore the plague has fallen on our dwellings, and the dead are more than the living in all our villages. Answer me, ye people, are not these things true?"

A hoarse sound of approval ran through the circle. A chant, in which the voices of the men and women blended, like the shrill wind in the pine-trees above the rumbling thunder of a waterfall, rose and fell in rude cadences.

O Thor, the Thunderer,
   Mighty and merciless,
   Spare us from smiting!
   Heave not thy hammer,
   Angry, against us;
   Plague not thy people.
   Take from our treasure
   Richest of ransom.
   Silver we send thee,
   Jewels and javelins,
   Goodliest garments,
   All our possessions,
   Priceless, we proffer.
   Sheep will we slaughter,
   Steeds will we sacrifice;
   Bright blood shall bathe thee,
   O tree of Thunder,
   Life-floods shall lave thee,

Strong wood of wonder.
Mighty, have mercy,
Smite us no more,
Spare us and save us,
Spare us, Thor! Thor!

With two great shouts the song ended, and a stillness followed so intense that the crackling of the fire
was heard distinctly. The old priest stood silent for a
moment. His shaggy brows swept down over his eyes
like ashes quenching flame. Then he lifted his face and
spoke.

"None of these things will please the god. More
costly is the offering that shall cleanse your sin, more
precious the crimson dew that shall send new life into
this holy tree of blood. Thor claims your dearest and
your noblest gift."

Hunrad moved nearer to the handful of children
who stood watching the red mines in the fire and the
swarms of spark-serpents darting upward. They had
heeded none of the priest's words, and did not notice
now that he approached them, so eager were they to
see which fiery snake would go highest among the oak
branches. Foremost among them, and most intent on
the pretty game, was a boy like a sunbeam, slender and
quick, with blithe brown eyes and laughing lips. The
priest's hand was laid upon his shoulder. The boy
turned and looked up in his face.

"Here," said the old man, with his voice vibrating
as when a thick rope is strained by a ship swinging from

her moorings, "here is the chosen one, the eldest son of the Chief, the darling of the people. Hearken, Bernhard, wilt thou go to Valhalla, where the heroes dwell with the gods, to bear a message to Thor?"

The boy answered, swift and clear:

"Yes, priest, I will go if my father bids me. Is it far away? Shall I run quickly? Must I take my bow and arrows for the wolves?"

The boy's father, the Chieftain Gundhar, standing among his bearded warriors, drew his breath deep, and leaned so heavily on the handle of his spear that the wood cracked. And his wife, Irma, bending forward from the ranks of women, pushed the golden hair from her forehead with one hand. The other dragged at the silver chain about her neck until the rough links pierced her flesh, and the red drops fell unheeded on the snow of her breast.

A sigh passed through the crowd, like the murmur of the forest before the storm breaks. Yet no one spoke save Hunrad:

"Yes, my Prince, both bow and spear shalt thou have, for the way is long, and thou art a brave huntsman. But in darkness thou must journey for a little space, and with eyes blindfolded. Fearest thou?"

"Naught fear I," said the boy, "neither darkness, nor the great bear, nor the were-wolf. For I am Gundhar's son, and the defender of my folk."

Then the priest led the child in his raiment of lamb's-wool to a broad stone in front of the fire. He gave him his little bow tipped with silver, and his spear with shining head of steel. He bound the child's eyes with a white cloth, and bade him kneel beside the stone with his face to the east. Unconsciously the wide arc of spectators drew inward toward the centre, as the ends of the bow draw together when the cord is stretched. Winfried moved noiselessly until he stood close behind the priest.

The old man stooped to lift a black hammer of stone from the ground,—the sacred hammer of the god Thor. Summoning all the strength of his withered arms, he swung it high in the air. It poised for an instant above the child's fair head—then turned to fall.

One keen cry shrilled out from where the women stood: "Me! take me! not Bernhard!"

The flight of the mother towards her child was swift as the falcon's swoop. But swifter still was the hand of the deliverer.

Winfried's heavy staff thrust mightily against the hammer's handle as it fell. Sideways it glanced from the old man's grasp, and the black stone, striking on the altar's edge, split in twain. A shout of awe and joy rolled along the living circle. The branches of the oak shivered. The flames leaped higher. As the shout died away the people saw the lady Irma, with her arms clasped round her child, and above them, on the altar-stone, Winfried, his face shining like the face of an angel.

❧ IV ❧
THE FELLING OF
THE TREE

4

A swift mountain-flood rolling down its channel; a huge rock tumbling from the hill-side and falling in mid-stream; the baffled waters broken and confused, pausing in their flow, dash high against the rock, foaming and murmuring, with divided impulse, uncertain whether to turn to the right or the left.

Even so Winfried's bold deed fell into the midst of the thoughts and passions of the council. They were at a standstill. Anger and wonder, reverence and joy and confusion surged through the crowd. They knew not which way to move: to resent the intrusion of the stranger as an insult to their gods, or to welcome him as the rescuer of their darling prince.

The old priest crouched by the altar, silent. Conflicting counsels troubled the air. Let the sacrifice go forward; the gods must be appeased. Nay, the boy must not die; bring the chieftain's best horse and slay it in his stead; it will be enough; the holy tree loves the blood of horses. Not so, there is a better counsel yet; seize the stranger whom the gods have led hither as a victim and make his life pay the forfeit of his daring.

The withered leaves on the oak rustled and whispered overhead. The fire flared and sank again. The angry voices clashed against each other and fell like opposing waves. Then the chieftain Gundhar struck the earth with his spear and gave his decision.

"All have spoken, but none are agreed. There is no voice of the council. Keep silence now, and let the stranger speak. His words shall give us judgment, whether he is to live or to die."

Winfried lifted himself high upon the altar, drew a roll of parchment from his bosom, and began to read.

"A letter from the great Bishop of Rome, who sits on a golden throne, to the people of the forest, Hessians and Thuringians, Franks and Saxons. *In nomine Domini, sanctae et individuae trinitatis, amen!*"

A murmur of awe ran through the crowd. "It is the sacred tongue of the Romans: the tongue that is heard and understood by the wise men of every land. There is magic in it. Listen!"

Winfried went on to read the letter, translating it into the speech of the people.

"'We have sent unto you our Brother Boniface, and appointed him your bishop, that he may teach you the only true faith, and baptize you, and lead you back from the ways of error to the path of salvation. Hearken to him in all things like a father. Bow your hearts to his teaching. He comes not for earthly gain, but for the gain of your souls. Depart from evil works. Worship not the false gods, for they are devils. Offer no more bloody sacrifices, nor eat the flesh of horses, but do as our Brother Boniface commands you. Build a house for him that he may dwell among you, and a church where you may offer your prayers to the only living God, the Almighty King of Heaven.'"

It was a splendid message: proud, strong, peaceful, loving. The dignity of the words imposed mightily upon the hearts of the people. They were quieted as men who have listened to a lofty strain of music.

"Tell us, then," said Gundhar, "what is the word that thou bringest to us from the Almighty. What is thy counsel for the tribes of the woodland on this night of sacrifice?"

"This is the word, and this is the counsel," answered Winfried. "Not a drop of blood shall fall to-night, save that which pity has drawn from the breast of your princess, in love for her child. Not a life shall be blotted out in the darkness tonight; but the great shadow of the tree which hides you from the light of heaven shall be swept away. For this is the birth-night of the white Christ, son of the All-Father, and Saviour of mankind. Fairer is He than Baldur the Beautiful, greater than Odin the Wise, kinder than Freya the Good. Since He has come to earth the bloody sacrifices must cease. The dark Thor, on whom you vainly call, is dead. Deep in the shades of Niffelheim he is lost forever. His power in the world is broken. Will you serve a helpless god? See, my brothers, you call this tree his oak. Does he dwell here? Does he protect it?"

A troubled voice of assent rose from the throng. The people stirred uneasily. Women covered their eyes. Hunrad lifted his head and muttered hoarsely, "Thor! take vengeance! Thor!"

Winfried beckoned to Gregor. "Bring the axes, thine and one for me. Now, young woodsman, show thy craft! The king-tree of the forest must fall, and swiftly, or all is lost!"

The two men took their places facing each other, one on each side of the oak. Their cloaks were flung aside, their heads bare. Carefully they felt the ground with their feet, seeking a firm grip of the earth. Firmly they grasped the axe-helves and swung the shining blades.

"Tree-god!" cried Winfried, "art thou angry? Thus we smite thee!"

"Tree-god!" answered Gregor, "art thou mighty? Thus we fight thee!"

Clang! clang! the alternate strokes beat time upon the hard, ringing wood. The axe-heads glittered in their rhythmic flight, like fierce eagles circling about their quarry.

The broad flakes of wood flew from the deepening gashes in the sides of the oak. The huge trunk quivered. There was a shuddering in the branches. Then the great wonder of Winfried's life came to pass.

Out of the stillness of the winter night, a mighty rushing noise sounded overhead.

Was it the ancient gods on their white battle-steeds, with their black hounds of wrath and their arrows of lightning, sweeping through the air to destroy their foes?

A strong, whirling wind passed over the tree-tops. It gripped the oak by its branches and tore it from its roots. Backward it fell, like a ruined tower, groaning and crashing as it split asunder in four great pieces.

Winfried let his axe drop, and bowed his head for a moment in the presence of almighty power.

Then he turned to the people, "Here is the timber," he cried, "already felled and split for your new building. On this spot shall rise a chapel to the true God and his servant St. Peter.

"And here," said he, as his eyes fell on a young fir-tree, standing straight and green, with its top pointing towards the stars, amid the divided ruins of the fallen oak, "here is the living tree, with no stain of blood upon it, that shall be the sign of your new worship. See how it points to the sky. Let us call it the tree of the Christ-child. Take it up and carry it to the chieftain's hall. You shall go no more into the shadows of the forest to keep your feasts with secret rites of shame. You shall keep them at home, with laughter and song and rites of love. The thunder-oak has fallen, and I think the day is coming when there shall not be a home in all Germany where the children are not gathered around the green fir-tree to rejoice in the birth-night of Christ."

So they took the little fir from its place, and carried

it in joyous procession to the edge of the glade, and laid it on the sledge. The horses tossed their heads and drew their load bravely, as if the new burden had made it lighter.

When they came to the house of Gundhar, he bade them throw open the doors of the hall and set the tree in the midst of it. They kindled lights among the branches until it seemed to be tangled full of fire-flies. The children encircled it, wondering, and the sweet odour of the balsam filled the house.

Then Winfried stood beside the chair of Gundhar, on the dais at the end of the hall, and told the story of Bethlehem; of the babe in the manger, of the shepherds on the hills, of the host of angels and their midnight song. All the people listened, charmed into stillness.

But the boy Bernhard, on Irma's knee, folded by her soft arm, grew restless as the story lengthened, and began to prattle softly at his mother's ear.

"Mother," whispered the child, "why did you cry out so loud, when the priest was going to send me to Valhalla?"

"Oh, hush, my child," answered the mother, and pressed him closer to her side.

"Mother," whispered the boy again, laying his finger on the stains upon her breast, "see, your dress is red! What are these stains? Did some one hurt you?"

The mother closed his mouth with a kiss. "Dear, be still, and listen!"

The boy obeyed. His eyes were heavy with sleep.

But he heard the last words of Winfried as he spoke of the angelic messengers, flying over the hills of Judea and singing as they flew. The child wondered and dreamed and listened. Suddenly his face grew bright. He put his lips close to Irma's cheek again.

"Oh, mother!" he whispered very low, "do not speak. Do you hear them? Those angels have come back again. They are singing now behind the tree."

And some say that it was true; but others say that it was only Gregor and his companions at the lower end of the hall, chanting their Christmas hymn:

> *All glory be to God on high,*
> *And to the earth be peace!*
> *Good-will, henceforth, from heaven to men*
> *Begin, and never cease.*

THE SPIRIT OF CHRISTMAS

A DREAM-STORY

THE CHRISTMAS ANGEL

It was the hour of rest in the Country Beyond the Stars. All the silver bells that swing with the turning of the great ring of light which lies around that land were softly chiming; and the sound of their commotion went down like dew upon the golden ways of the city, and the long alleys of blossoming trees, and the meadows of asphodel, and the curving shores of the River of Life.

At the hearing of that chime, all the angels who had been working turned to play, and all who had been playing gave themselves joyfully to work. Those who had been singing, and making melody on different instruments, fell silent and began to listen. Those who had been walking alone in meditation met together in companies to talk. And those who had been far away on errands to the Earth and other planets came homeward like a flight of swallows to the high cliff when the day is over.

It was not that they needed to be restored from weariness, for the inhabitants of that country never say, "I am tired." But there, as here, the law of change is the secret of happiness, and the joy that never ends is woven of mingled strands of labour and repose, society and solitude, music and silence. Sleep comes to them not as it does to us, with a darkening of the vision and a folding of the wings of the spirit, but with an opening of the eyes to deeper and fuller light, and with an effortless outgoing of the soul upon broader currents of life, as the sun-loving bird poises and circles upward, without a wing-beat, on the upholding air.

It was in one of the quiet corners of the green valley called Peacefield, where the little brook of Brighthopes runs smoothly down to join the River of Life, that I saw a company of angels, returned from various labours on Earth, sitting in friendly converse on the hill-side, where cyclamens and arbutus and violets and fringed orchids and pale lady's-tresses, and all the sweet-smelling flowers which are separated in the lower world by the seasons, were thrown together in a harmony of fragrance. There were three of the company who seemed to be leaders, distinguished not only by more radiant and powerful looks, but by a tone of authority in their speech and by the willing attention with which the others listened to them, as they talked of their earthly tasks, of the tangles and troubles, the wars and miseries that they had seen among men, and of the best way to get rid of them and bring sorrow to an end.

"The Earth is full of oppression and unrighteous-ness," said the tallest and most powerful of the angels. His voice was deep and strong, and by his shining armour and the long two-handed sword hanging over his shoulder I knew that he was the archangel Michael, the mightiest one among the warriors of the King, and the executor of the divine judgments upon the unjust. "The Earth is tormented with injustice," he cried, "and the great misery that I have seen among men is that the evil hand is often stronger than the good hand and can beat it down.

"The arm of the cruel is heavier than the arm of the kind. The unjust get the better of the just and tread on them. I have seen tyrant kings crush their helpless folk. I have seen the fields of the innocent trampled into bloody ruin by the feet of conquering armies. I have seen the wicked nation overcome the peoples that loved liberty, and take away their treasure by force of arms. I have seen poverty mocked by arrogant wealth, and purity deflowered by brute violence, and gentleness and fair-dealing bruised in the winepress of iniquity and pride.

"There is no cure for this evil, but by the giving of greater force to the good hand. The righteous cause must be strengthened with might to resist the wicked, to defend the helpless, to punish all cruelty and unfair-ness, to uphold the right everywhere, and to enforce justice with unconquerable arms. Oh, that the host of Heaven might be called, arrayed, and sent to mingle in the wars of men, to make the good victorious, to destroy all evil, and to make the will of the King prevail!

"We would shake down the thrones of tyrants, and loose the bands of the oppressed. We would hold the cruel and violent with the bit of fear, and drive the greedy and fierce-minded men with the whip of terror. We would stand guard, with weapons drawn, about the innocent, the gentle, the kind, and keep the peace of God with the sword of the angels!"

As he spoke, his hands were lifted to the hilt of his long blade, and he raised it above him, straight and shining, throwing sparkles of light around it, like the spray from the sharp prow of a moving ship. Bright flames of heavenly ardour leaped in the eyes of the listening angels; a martial air passed over their faces as if they longed for the call to war.

But no silver trumpet blared from the battlements of the City of God; no crimson flag was unfurled on those high, secret walls; no thrilling drum-beat echoed over the smooth meadow. Only the sound of the brook of Brighthopes was heard tinkling and murmuring among the roots of the grasses and flowers; and far off a cadence of song drifted down from the inner courts of the Palace of the King.

Then another angel began to speak, and made answer to Michael. He, too, was tall and wore the look of power. But it was power of the mind rather than of the hand. His face was clear and glistening, and his eyes were lit with a steady flame which neither leaped nor fell. Of flame also were his garments, which clung about him as the fire enwraps a torch burning where there is no wind; and his great wings, spiring to a point far above his head, were like a living lamp before the altar of the Most High. By this sign I knew that it was the archangel Uriel, the spirit of the Sun, clearest in vision, deepest in wisdom of all the spirits that surround the throne.

"I hold not the same thought," said he, "as the great archangel Michael; nor, though I desire the same end which he desires, would I seek it by the same way. For I know how often power has been given to the good, and how often it has been turned aside and used for evil. I know that the host of Heaven, and the very stars in their courses, have fought on the side of a favoured nation; yet pride has followed triumph and oppression has been the first-born child of victory. I know that the deliverers of the people have become tyrants over those whom they have set free, and the fighters for liberty have been changed into the soldiers of fortune. Power corrupts itself, and might cannot save.

"Does not the Prince Michael remember how the angel of the Lord led the armies of Israel, and gave them the battle against every foe, except the enemy within the camp? And how they robbed and crushed the peoples against whom they had fought for freedom? And how the wickedness of the tribes of Canaan survived their conquest and overcame their conquerors, so that the children of Israel learned to worship the idols of their enemies, Moloch, and Baal, and Ashtoreth?

"Power corrupts itself, and might cannot save. Was not Persia the destroyer of Babylon, and did not the tyranny of Persia cry aloud for destruction? Did not Rome break the yoke of the East, and does not the yoke of Rome lie heavy on the shoulders of the world? Listen!"

There was silence for a moment on the slopes of Peacefield, and then over the encircling hills a cool wind brought the sound of chains clanking in prisons and galleys, the sighing of millions of slaves, the weeping of wretched women and children, the blows of hammers nailing men to their crosses. Then the sound passed by with the wind, and Uriel spoke again:

"Power corrupts itself, and might cannot save. The Earth is full of ignorant strife, and for this evil there is no cure but by the giving of greater knowledge. It is because men do not understand evil that they yield themselves to its power. Wickedness is folly in action, and injustice is the error of the blind. It is because men are ignorant that they destroy one another, and at last themselves.

"If there were more light in the world there would be no sorrow. If the great King who knows all things would enlighten the world with wisdom—wisdom to understand his law and his ways, to read the secrets of the earth and the stars, to discern the workings of the heart of man and the things that make for joy and peace—if he would but send us, his messengers, as a flame of fire to shine upon those who sit in darkness, how gladly would we go to bring in the new day!

"We would speak the word of warning and counsel to the erring, and tell knowledge to the perplexed. We would guide the ignorant in the paths of prudence, and the young would sit at our feet and hear us gladly in the school of life. Then folly would fade away as the morning vapour, and the sun of wisdom would shine on all men, and the peace of God would come with the counsel of the angels."

A murmur of pleasure followed the words of Uriel, and eager looks flashed around the circle of the messengers of light as they heard the praise of wisdom fitly spoken. But there was one among them on whose face a shadow of doubt rested, and though he smiled, it was as if he remembered something that the others had forgotten. He turned to an angel near him.

"Who was it," said he, "to whom you were sent with counsel long ago? Was it not Balaam the son of Beor, as he was riding to meet the King of Moab? And did not even the dumb beast profit more by your instruction than the man who rode him? And who was it," he continued, turning to Uriel, "that was called the wisest of all men, having searched out and understood the many inventions that are found under the sun? Was not Solomon, prince of fools and philosophers, unable by much learning to escape weariness of the flesh and despair of the spirit? Knowledge also is vanity and vexation. This I know well, because I have dwelt among men and held converse with them since the day when I was sent to instruct the first man in Eden."

Then I looked more closely at him who was speaking and recognised the beauty of the archangel Raphael, as it was pictured long ago:

"A seraph winged; six wings he wore to shade
His lineaments divine; the pair that clad
Each shoulder broad came mantling o'er his breast,
With regal ornament; the middle pair
Girt like a starry zone his waist, and round
Skirted his loins and thighs with downy gold
And colours dipped in Heav'n; the third his feet
Shadowed from either heel with feathered mail,
Sky-tinctured grain. Like Maia's son he stood
And shook his plumes, that Heavenly fragrance filled
The circuit wide."

"Too well I know," he spoke on, while the smile on his face deepened into a look of pity and tenderness and desire, "too well I know that power corrupts itself and that knowledge cannot save. There is no cure for the evil that is in the world but by the giving of more love to men. The laws that are ordained for earth are strange and unequal, and the ways where men must walk are full of pitfalls and dangers. Pestilence creeps along the ground and flows in the rivers; whirlwind and tempest shake the habitations of men and drive their ships to destruction; fire breaks forth from the mountains and the foundations of the world tremble. Frail is the flesh of man, and many are his pains and troubles. His children can never find peace until they learn to love one another and to help one another.

"Wickedness is begotten by disease and misery. Violence comes from poverty and hunger. The cruelty of oppression is when the strong tread the weak under their feet; the bitterness of pride is when the wise and learned despise the simple; the crown of folly is when the rich think they are gods, and the poor think that God is not.

"Hatred and envy and contempt are the curse of life. And for these there is no remedy save love—the will to give and to bless—the will of the King himself, who gives to all and is loving unto every man. But how shall the hearts of men be won to this will? How shall it enter into them and possess them? Even the gods that men fashion for themselves are cruel and proud and false and unjust. How shall the miracle be wrought in human nature to reveal the meaning of humanity? How shall men be made like God?"

At this question a deep hush fell around the circle, and every listener was still, even as the rustling leaves hang motionless when the light breeze falls away in the hour of sunset. Then through the silence, like the song of a far-away thrush from its hermitage in the forest, a voice came ringing: "I know it, I know it, I know it."

Clear and sweet—clear as a ray of light, sweeter than the smallest silver bell that rang the hour of rest— was that slender voice floating on the odorous and translucent air. Nearer and nearer it came, echoing down the valley, "I know it, I know it, I know it!"

Then from between the rounded hills, among which the brook of Brighthopes is born, appeared a young angel, a little child, with flying hair of gold, and green wreaths twined about his shoulders, and fluttering hands that played upon the air and seemed to lift him so lightly that he had no need of wings. As thistledown, blown by the wind, dances across the water, so he came along the little stream, singing clear above the murmur of the brook.

All the angels rose and turned to look at him with wondering eyes. Multitudes of others came flying swiftly to the place from which the strange, new song was sounding. Rank within rank, like a garden of living flowers, they stood along the sloping banks of the brook while the child-angel floated into the midst of them, singing:

"I know it, I know it, I know it! Man shall be made like God because the Son of God shall become a man."

At this all the angels looked at one another with amazement, and gathered more closely about the child-angel, as those who hear wonderful news.

"How can this be?" they asked. "How is it possible that the Son of God should be a man?"

"I do not know," said the young angel. "I only know that it is to be."

"But if he becomes a man," said Raphael, "he will be at the mercy of men; the cruel and the wicked will have power upon him; he will suffer."

"I know it," answered the young angel, "and by suffering he will understand the meaning of all sorrow and pain; and he will be able to comfort every one who cries; and his own tears will be for the healing of sad hearts; and those who are healed by him will learn for his sake to be kind to each other."

"But if the Son of God is a true man," said Uriel, "he must first be a child, simple, and lowly, and helpless. It may be that he will never gain the learning of the schools. The masters of earthly wisdom will despise him and speak scorn of him."

"I know it," said the young angel, "but in meekness will he answer them; and to those who become as little children he will give the heavenly wisdom that comes, without seeking, to the pure and gentle of heart."

"But if he becomes a man," said Michael, "evil men will hate and persecute him: they may even take his life, if they are stronger than he."

"I know it," answered the young angel, "they will nail him to a cross. But when he is lifted up, he will draw all men unto him, for he will still be the Son of God, and no heart that is open to love can help loving him, since his love for men is so great that he is willing to die for them."

"But how do you know these things?" cried the other angels. "Who are you?"

"I am the Christmas angel," he said. "At first I was sent as the dream of a little child, a holy child, blessed and wonderful, to dwell in the heart of a pure virgin, Mary of Nazareth. There I was hidden till the word came to call me back to the throne of the King, and tell me my name, and give me my new message. For this is Christmas day on Earth, and to-day the Son of God is born of a woman. So I must fly quickly, before the sun rises, to bring the good news to those happy men who have been chosen to receive them."

As he said this, the young angel rose, with arms outspread, from the green meadow of Peacefield and, passing over the bounds of Heaven, dropped swiftly as a shooting-star toward the night shadow of the Earth. The other angels followed him—a throng of dazzling forms, beautiful as a rain of jewels falling from the dark-blue sky. But the child-angel went more swiftly than the others, because of the certainty of gladness in his heart.

And as the others followed him they wondered who had been favoured and chosen to receive the glad tidings.

"It must be the Emperor of the World and his counsellors," they thought. But the flight passed over Rome.

"It may be the philosophers and the masters of learning," they thought. But the flight passed over Athens.

"Can it be the High Priest of the Jews, and the elders and the scribes?" they thought. But the flight passed over Jerusalem.

It floated out over the hill country of Bethlehem; the throng of silent angels holding close together, as if perplexed and doubtful; the child-angel darting on far in advance, as one who knew the way through the darkness.

The villages were all still: the very houses seemed asleep; but in one place there was a low sound of talking in a stable, near to an inn—a sound as of a mother soothing her baby to rest.

All over the pastures on the hillsides a light film of snow had fallen, delicate as the veil of a bride adorned for the marriage; and as the child-angel passed over them, alone in the swiftness of his flight, the pure fields sparkled round him, giving back his radiance.

And there were in that country shepherds abiding in the fields, keeping watch over their flocks by night. And lo! the angel of the Lord came upon them, and the glory of the Lord shone round about them, and they were sore afraid. And the angel said unto them: "Fear not; for behold I bring you glad tidings of great joy which shall be to all nations. For unto you is born this day, in the city of David, a Saviour, which is Christ the Lord. And this shall be a sign unto you; ye shall find the babe wrapped in swaddling clothes, lying in a manger."

And suddenly there was with the angel a multitude of the heavenly host, praising God and saying: "Glory to God in the highest, and on earth peace, good-will toward men." And the shepherds said one to another: "Let us now go, even to Bethlehem, and see this thing which is come to pass."

So I said within myself that I also would go with the shepherds, even to Bethlehem. And I heard a great and sweet voice, as of a bell, which said, "Come!" And when the bell had sounded twelve times, I awoke; and it was Christmas morn; and I knew that I had been in a dream.

Yet it seemed to me that the things which I had heard were true.

A LITTLE ESSAY

CHRISTMAS-GIVING AND CHRISTMAS-LIVING

I.

The custom of exchanging presents on a certain day in the year is very much older than Christmas, and means very much less. It has obtained in almost all ages of the world, and among many different nations. It is a fine thing or a foolish thing, as the case may be; an encouragement to friendliness, or a tribute to fashion; an expression of good nature, or a bid for favour; an outgoing of generosity, or a disguise of greed; a cheerful old custom, or a futile old farce, according to the spirit which animates it and the form which it takes.

But when this ancient and variously interpreted tradition of a day of gifts was transferred to the Christmas season, it was brought into vital contact with an idea which must transform it, and with an example which must lift it up to a higher plane. The example is the life of Jesus. The idea is unselfish interest in the happiness of others.

The great gift of Jesus to the world was himself. He lived with and for men. He kept back nothing. In every particular and personal gift that he made to certain people there was something of himself that made it precious.

For example, at the wedding in Cana of Galilee, it was his thought for the feelings of the giver of the feast, and his wish that every guest should find due entertainment, that lent the flavour of a heavenly hospitality to the wine which he provided.

When he gave bread and fish to the hungry multitude who had followed him out among the hills by the Lake of Gennesaret, the people were refreshed and strengthened by the sense of the personal care of Jesus for their welfare, as much as by the food which he bestowed upon them. It was another illustration of the sweetness of "a dinner of herbs, where love is."

The gifts of healing which he conferred upon many different kinds of sufferers were, in every case, evidences that Jesus was willing to give something of himself, his thought, his sympathy, his vital power, to the men and women among whom he lived. Once, when a paralytic was brought to Jesus on a bed, he surprised everybody, and offended many, by giving the poor wretch the pardon of his sins, before he gave new life to his body. That was just because Jesus thought before he gave; because he desired to satisfy the deepest need; because in fact he gave something of himself in every gift. All true Christmas-giving ought to be after this pattern.

Not that it must all be solemn and serious. For the most part it deals with little wants, little joys, little tokens of friendly feeling. But the feeling must be more than the token; else the gift does not really belong to Christmas.

It takes time and effort and unselfish expenditure of strength to make gifts in this way. But it is the only way that fits the season.

The finest Christmas gift is not the one that costs the most money, but the one that carries the most love.

II.

But how seldom Christmas comes—only once a year; and how soon it is over—a night and a day! If that is the whole of it, it seems not much more durable than the little toys that one buys of a fakir on the street-corner. They run for an hour, and then the spring breaks, and the legs come off, and nothing remains but a contribution to the dust heap.

But surely that need not and ought not to be the whole of Christmas—only a single day of generosity, ransomed from the dull servitude of a selfish year,—only a single night of merry-making, celebrated in the slave-quarters of a selfish race! If every gift is the token of a personal thought, a friendly feeling, an unselfish interest in the joy of others, then the thought, the feeling, the interest, may remain after the gift is made.

The little present, or the rare and long-wished-for gift (it matters not whether the vessel be of gold, or silver, or iron, or wood, or clay, or just a small bit of birch bark folded into a cup), may carry a message something like this:

"I am thinking of you to-day, because it is Christmas, and I wish you happiness. And to-morrow, because it will be the day after Christmas, I shall still wish you happiness; and so on, clear through the year. I may not be able to tell you about it every day, because I may be far away; or because both of us may be very busy; or perhaps because I cannot even afford to pay the postage on so many letters, or find the time to write them. But that makes no difference. The thought and the wish will be here just the same. In my work and in the business of life, I mean to try not to be unfair to you or injure you in any way. In my pleasure, if we can be together, I would like to share the fun with you. Whatever joy or success comes to you will make me glad. Without pretense, and in plain words, good-will to you is what I mean, in the Spirit of Christmas."

It is not necessary to put a message like this into high-flown language, to swear absolute devotion and deathless consecration. In love and friendship, small, steady payments on a gold basis are better than immense promissory notes. Nor, indeed, is it always necessary to put the message into words at all, nor even to convey it by a tangible token. To feel it and to act it out—that is the main thing.

There are a great many people in the world whom

we know more or less, but to whom for various reasons we cannot very well send a Christmas gift. But there is hardly one, in all the circles of our acquaintance, with whom we may not exchange the touch of Christmas life.

In the outer circles, cheerful greetings, courtesy, consideration; in the inner circles, sympathetic interest, hearty congratulations, honest encouragement; in the inmost circle, comradeship, helpfulness, tenderness,—

"Beautiful friendship tried by sun and wind
Durable from the daily dust of life."

After all, Christmas-living is the best kind of Christmas-giving.

A SHORT CHRISTMAS SERMON

KEEPING CHRISTMAS

He that regardeth the day, regardeth it unto the Lord.

— ROMANS, XIV, 6

It is a good thing to observe Christmas day. The mere marking of times and seasons, when men agree to stop work and make merry together, is a wise and wholesome custom. It helps one to feel the supremacy of the common life over the individual life. It reminds a man to set his own little watch, now and then, by the great clock of humanity which runs on sun time.

But there is a better thing than the observance of Christmas day, and that is, keeping Christmas.

Are you willing to forget what you have done for other people, and to remember what other people have done for you; to ignore what the world owes you, and to think what you owe the world; to put your rights in the background, and your duties in the middle distance, and your chances to do a little more than your duty in the foreground; to see that your fellow-men are just as real as you are, and try to look behind their faces to their hearts, hungry for joy; to own that probably the only good reason for your existence is not what you are going to get out of life, but what you are going to give to life; to close your book of complaints against the management of the universe, and look around you for a place where you can sow a few seeds of happiness— are you willing to do these things even for a day? Then you can keep Christmas.

Are you willing to stoop down and consider the needs and the desires of little children; to remember the weakness and loneliness of people who are growing old; to stop asking how much your friends love you, and ask yourself whether you love them enough; to bear in mind the things that other people have to bear on their hearts; to try to understand what those who live in the same house with you really want, without waiting for them to tell you; to trim your lamp so that it will give more light and less smoke, and to carry it in front so that your shadow will fall behind you; to make a grave for your ugly thoughts, and a garden for your kindly feelings, with the gate open—are you willing to do these things even for a day? Then you can keep Christmas.

Are you willing to believe that love is the strongest thing in the world—stronger than hate, stronger than evil, stronger than death—and that the blessed life which began in Bethlehem nineteen hundred years ago is the image and brightness of the Eternal Love? Then you can keep Christmas.

And if you keep it for a day, why not always?

But you can never keep it alone.

TWO CHRISTMAS PRAYERS

A CHRISTMAS PRAYER FOR THE HOME

Father of all men, look upon our family,
Kneeling together before Thee,
And grant us a true Christmas.

With loving heart we bless Thee:
For the gift of Thy dear Son Jesus Christ,
For the peace He brings to human homes,
For the good-will He teaches to sinful men,
For the glory of Thy goodness shining in His
    face.

With joyful voice we praise Thee:
For His lowly birth and His rest in the manger,
For the pure tenderness of His mother Mary,
For the fatherly care that protected Him,
For the Providence that saved the Holy Child
To be the Saviour of the world.

With deep desire we beseech Thee:
Help us to keep His birthday truly,
Help us to offer, in His name, our Christmas
    prayer.
From the sickness of sin and the darkness of
    doubt,
From selfish pleasures and sullen pains,
From the frost of pride and the fever of envy,
God save us every one, through the blessing of
    Jesus.
In the health of purity and the calm of mutual
    trust,
In the sharing of joy and the bearing of trouble,
In the steady glow of love and the clear light of
    hope,
God keep us every one, by the blessing of Jesus.

In praying and praising, in giving and receiving,
In eating and drinking, in singing and making
    merry,
In parents' gladness and in children's mirth,
In dear memories of those who have departed,
In good comradeship with those who are here,
In kind wishes for those who are far away,
In patient waiting, sweet contentment, generous
    cheer,
God bless us every one, with the blessing of
    Jesus.

By remembering our kinship with all men,

By well-wishing, friendly speaking and kindly
   doing,
By cheering the downcast and adding sunshine
   to daylight,
By welcoming strangers (poor shepherds or wise
   men),
By keeping the music of the angels' song in this
   home,
God help us every one to share the blessing of
   Jesus:
In whose name we keep Christmas:
And in whose words we pray together:

Our Father which art in heaven, hallowed be Thy name.
Thy kingdom come. Thy will be done in earth, as it is in
   heaven.
Give us this day our daily bread. And forgive us our
   debts, as we forgive our debtors.
And lead us not into temptation, but deliver us from evil:
For Thine is the kingdom, and the power, and the glory,
   forever. Amen.

A CHRISTMAS PRAYER FOR
LONELY FOLKS

Lord God of the solitary,
Look upon me in my loneliness.
Since I may not keep this Christmas in the
      home,
Send it into my heart.

Let not my sins cloud me in,
But shine through them with forgiveness in the
      face of the child Jesus.
Put me in loving remembrance of the lowly
      lodging in the stable of Bethlehem,
The sorrows of the blessed Mary, the poverty
      and exile of the Prince of Peace.
For His sake, give me a cheerful courage to
      endure my lot,
And an inward comfort to sweeten it.

Purge my heart from hard and bitter thoughts.

Let no shadow of forgetting come between me
    and friends far away:
Bless them in their Christmas mirth:
Hedge me in with faithfulness,
That I may not grow unworthy to meet them
    again.

Give me good work to do,
That I may forget myself and find peace in
    doing it for Thee.
Though I am poor, send me to carry some gift
    to those who are poorer,
Some cheer to those who are more lonely.
Grant me the joy to do a kindness to one of
    Thy little ones:
Light my Christmas candle at the gladness of
    an innocent and grateful heart.

Strange is the path where Thou leadest me:
Let me not doubt Thy wisdom, nor lose Thy
    hand.
Make me sure that Eternal Love is revealed in
    Jesus, Thy dear Son,
To save us from sin and solitude and death.
Teach me that I am not alone,
But that many hearts, all round the world,
Join with me through the silence, while I pray in
    His name:

Our Father which art in heaven, hallowed be Thy name.

*Thy kingdom come. Thy will be done in earth, as it is in
     heaven.*
*Give us this day our daily bread. And forgive us our
     debts, as we forgive our debtors.*
And lead us not into temptation, but deliver us from evil:
*For Thine is the kingdom, and the power, and the glory,
     forever. Amen.*

Made in United States
Troutdale, OR
08/07/2024

21839449R00083